characters created by

lauren child

I am really, REALLY
Concentrating

Grosset & Dunlap

Text based on the script written by Samantha Hill

Illustrations from the TV animation produced by Tiger Aspect

GROSSET & DUNLAP
Published by the Penguin Group
Penguin Group (USA) Inc., 375 Hudson Street, New York, New York 10014, USA
Penguin Group (Canada), 90 Eglinton Avenue East, Suite 700, Toronto, Ontario M4P 2Y3, Canada
(a division of Pearson Penguin Canada Inc.)
Penguin Books Ltd., 80 Strand, London WC2R 0RL, England
Penguin Group Ireland, 25 St. Stephen's Green, Dublin 2, Ireland
(a division of Penguin Books Ltd.)
Penguin Group (Australia), 250 Camberwell Road, Camberwell, Victoria 3124, Australia
(a division of Pearson Australia Group Pty. Ltd.)
Penguin Books India Pvt. Ltd., 11 Community Centre, Panchsheel Park, New Delhi—110 017, India
Penguin Group (NZ), 67 Apollo Drive, Rosedale, North Shore 0632, New Zealand
(a division of Pearson New Zealand Ltd.)
Penguin Books (South Africa) (Pty.) Ltd., 24 Sturdee Avenue,
Rosebank, Johannesburg 2196, South Africa

Penguin Books Ltd., Registered Offices: 80 Strand, London WC2R 0RL, England

Library of Congress Cataloging-in-Publication Data is available.

ISBN 978-0-448-44905-0

I have this little sister, Lola.
She is small and very funny.
            Lola is very excited because
it's almost Field Day.
            And this is Lola's first ever Field Day.

Lola asks,
"What do you do
            on Field Day?"

And I say,
        "There are all sorts
of races . . . like **running**."

        "I don't like **running**."

So I say,
        "There's also **jumping**."

"Not **jumping**, Charlie.
        My legs are quite short."

Then I say,
"Let's go to the park
        to practice some **games**
with Lotta and Marv."

At the park, I say,
"Let's try the
three-legged race."

Lola says,
"That sounds easy-peasy!"

"Easy-peasy-
lemon-squeezy!"
says Lotta.

Then I say, "Maybe we
should try the **obstacle** race?"

"Oc-to-pus race?" asks Lola.

And I say,
"No, an **ob-sta-cle** race.
You **run** twice
around the boot, **skip** twice
with the **jump** rope,
do two circles with the
hula hoop, and
bounce the ball
on the racket.

On your mark,
get set, GO!"

Lotta crosses
the finish line first.
But Lola is a bit
more slow.

Lotta says, "I think the
oᶜ-tᵒ-pᵘs race is
the very best!"

Marv says,
"Well done, Lotta. You'll be
really good at Field Day.
But what about Lola?"

Later Lola says,
"I still don't know
what **race** to do."

And I say, "I know!
The **egg**-and-**spoon** race!"

Lola says, "Yes!
Because I love **eggs**
and I love **spoons**!

Charlie,
what is the **egg**-
and-**spoon** race?"

I say, "It's when you
run a race
balancing an **egg**
on a **spoon**."

So Lola practices . . .

and practices . . .

. . . and soon she says,

"Look, Charlie!
I am a champion
egg and **Spooner!**"

So I ask,
"Lola, did you glue
the **egg** to the **spoon**?"

"Yes, Charlie. Now it
doesn't fall off!"

So I say,
"But glue is **cheating**."

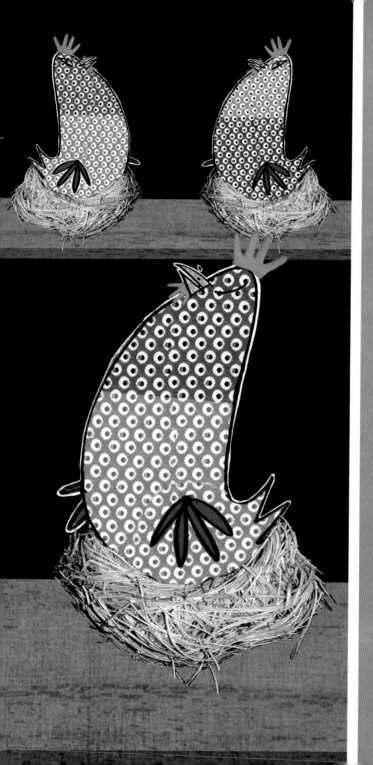

"Then I need to find
an **egg** that's not all **wobbly**.
A perfect **egg**
from a perfect chicken
that I will never EVER drop."

I say,
"But it's okay to **drop** it.
You just have
to put it back on the **spoon**
and keep going."

But Lola says,
"No, Charlie. I do not
want to drop this **egg**
because it is
completely perfect."

Later Lola says,
        "Oh, I'm NEVER
going to get the **egg**
        to stay on my **SpoOn**."

So I say,
"You will! You just
        have to **concentrate**.
        Don't take your
eyes off it for one
        single minute.
        Do you understand?"

        Lola says,
"Oh, I can **CoN-cen-trAte**.
        I know I can, Charlie."

At Field Day
me and Marv
do the **three-legged** race.

Lotta does the
obstacle race,
and then it's Lola's turn.

I shout,
"CONCENTRATE, Lola!"

Marv shouts,
"You can do it, Lola!"

Then Lotta says,
"She's not going
                very **fast**, is she?"

And I say,
"Oh dear . . .
                She is **last**."

But after the race Lola says,
"Look! Mrs. Hanson gave me an ever so special ribbon
because my **egg** did not fall off
my **spoon** even **one single** time!"